Forest Stew

by Nita Shah
illustrated by Tim Bowers

 HOUGHTON MIFFLIN HARCOURT
School Publishers

Copyright © by Houghton Mifflin Harcourt Publishing Company

Printed in China

ISBN-13: 978-0-547-02869-9
ISBN-10: 0-547-02869-5

5 6 7 8 0940 18 17 16 15 14 13 12
4500358727

Skunk put her big pot
on the stove.
She thought to herself,
"I'm so hungry! I'll make my
favorite stew."

Skunk put some beans in the pot.
She put an onion in the pot.
She put a potato in the pot.
She tasted the stew.
"It doesn't taste good!" she cried.
She called her friends to ask
for help.

"I make great stew,"
Skunk told her friends.
"But today it's missing something."
Dog said, "Put in some rice."
So Skunk put in some rice.

4

"Put in some carrots,"
said Rabbit.
So Skunk put in some carrots.
She mixed the stew and tasted it.
"It's getting better," Skunk said.

"I know what is missing,"
said Bear.
"Put in some honey."
So Skunk added a bit of honey.

The pot was getting full
and the stew had turned gray.
But it didn't taste good.
Skunk started to worry.

Then Skunk looked
out her window and saw her
herb garden.
"I forgot to add spice!" she
yelled. She ran outside and
picked some spice.
She put the spice in the stew.

Skunk gave her friends
some of the stew.
"Wow!" said Dog.
"You're a pretty good cook!"
 "Thanks," Skunk said.
"My friends helped me
make a great stew!"

"This stew has all our favorite
foods in it," Rabbit said.
"I suggest we call this
Forest Stew!" roared Bear.
Then Skunk and her friends stayed
up all night, eating Forest Stew.

Responding

Story Structure

Who is this story about? Where does the story happen? What happens in the story? Make a chart.

Write About It

Text to Text Think of a different story about food. Draw a picture of the food in the story. Write two sentences to tell what happens in the story.

better	**thought**
night	**told**
pretty	**turned**
saw	**window**

✔ **TARGET SKILL** Story Structure

Tell the setting, character, and events in a story.

✔ **TARGET STRATEGY** Analyze/Evaluate

Tell how you feel about the text, and why.

GENRE A **fantasy** is a story that could not happen in real life.